Nat the Cat
Has a Snack

By Jarrett Lerner

Ready-to-Read

Simon Spotlight
New York   London   Toronto   Sydney   New Delhi

For Steph

SIMON SPOTLIGHT
An imprint of Simon & Schuster Children's Publishing Division
1230 Avenue of the Americas, New York, New York 10020
This Simon Spotlight edition May 2024
Copyright © 2024 by Jarrett Lerner
All rights reserved, including the right of reproduction
in whole or in part in any form.
SIMON SPOTLIGHT, READY-TO-READ, and colophon
are registered trademarks of Simon & Schuster, LLC.
Simon & Schuster: Celebrating 100 Years of Publishing in 2024
For information about special discounts for bulk purchases,
please contact Simon & Schuster Special Sales at 1-866-506-1949
or business@simonandschuster.com.
Manufactured in the United States of America 0324 LAK
2 4 6 7 10 9 7 5 3 1
This book has been cataloged by the Library of Congress.
ISBN 978-1-6659-5709-0 (hc)
ISBN 978-1-6659-5708-3 (pbk)
ISBN 978-1-6659-5710-6 (ebook)

This is Nat.

Nat is a cat.

Nat the Cat is having a snack.

This is Pat.
Pat is a rat.

Does Pat the Rat like snacks?

Perfect!
Nat the Cat
has a snack.

Oh no!
Pat the Rat
is sad.

Wait!
Nat the Cat
can SHARE
his snack!

Uh-oh.

Yikes!

Watch out, Nat!